D1341710

First published in Great Britain 2022 by Farshore
An imprint of HarperCollins*Publishers,*
1 London Bridge Street, London SE1 9GF
www.farshore.co.uk

HarperCollins*Publishers* 1st Floor, Watermarque Building, Ringsend Road Dublin 4, Ireland

Written by Laura Jackson.

© 2022 Disney Enterprises, Inc.
The movie THE PRINCESS AND THE FROG copyright © 2009, Disney, inspired in part by the book
THE FROG PRINCE by E. D. Baker copyright © 2002, published by Bloomsbury Publishing, Inc.

ISBN 978 0 0085 0763 3
Printed in Romania
001
A CIP catalogue record for this title is available from the British Library.

Parental guidance is advised for all craft and colouring activities. Always ask an adult to help
when using glue, paint and scissors. Wear protective clothing and cover surfaces to avoid staining.

Stay safe online. Farshore is not responsible for content hosted by third parties.

**MIX**
Paper from
responsible sources
FSC™ C007454
FSC
www.fsc.org

## This
# Disney Princess
## Annual 2023 belongs to

......................Bethan......................

..................................................

## Age .....................

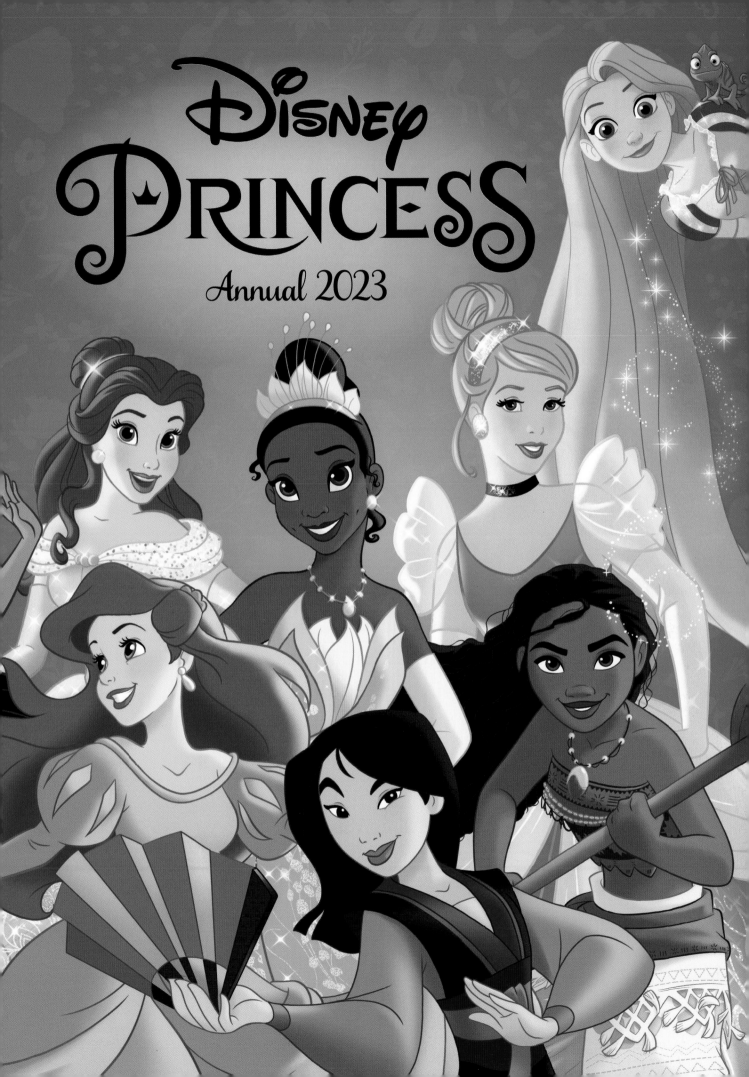

# Disney PRINCESS

### Annual 2023

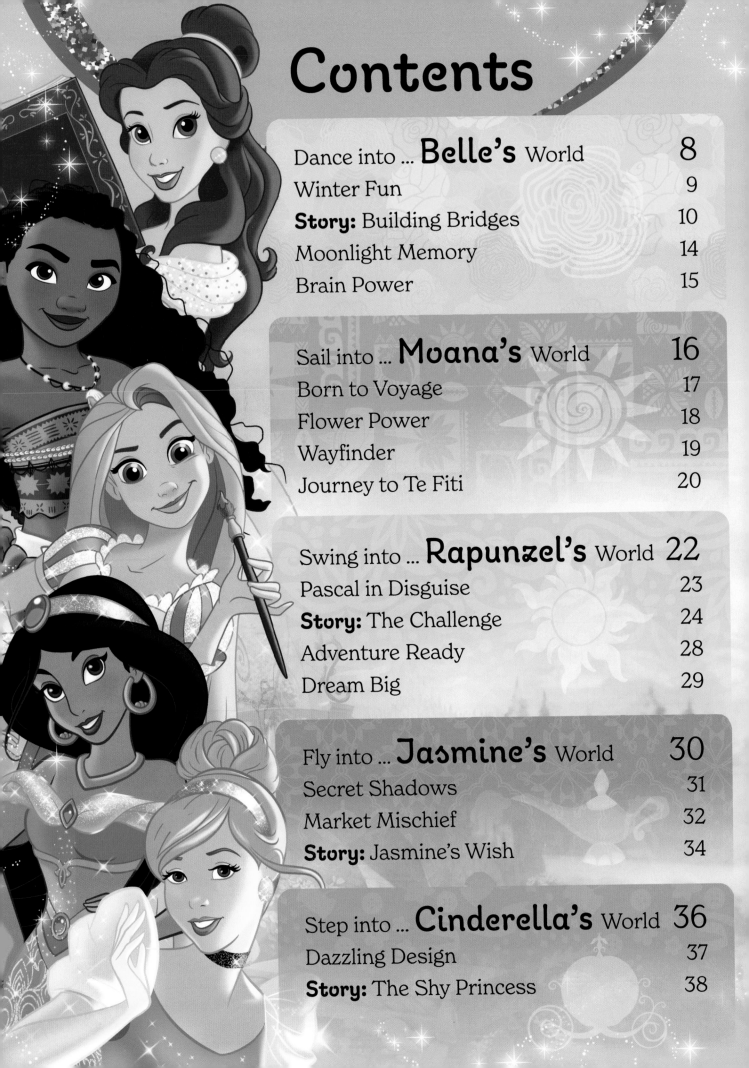

# Contents

# Dance into ...
# Belle's World!

When **Belle** isn't busy reading, she is usually helping somebody. When nobody in her town can see the good in the Beast, Belle bravely stands by him. She saves his life and finds true love and friendship.

Best friend ...
her trusty horse, Phillipe.

Secrets and dreams ...
to have adventures far, far away.

Strengths ...
clever and sees the best in everyone.

Loves ...
reading and inventing things.

There is
## magic
in a book!

# Winter Fun

Belle loves to slip and slide across the ice. Trace her frosty trail. Now colour her dress in your favourite winter colours.

# Building Bridges

**1** One morning, Belle was shopping in the village square when she came across a poster for a contest! Belle thought a contest sounded like fun!

**2** The poster said that the bridge across the river was too low for boats to pass under. The town elders would give a prize to whoever could design a new bridge to solve the problem.

**3** "Hello, Belle," said Gaston. "Guess who is going to win this contest?" "I don't know," said Belle, "but I read about a bridge that could open for boats and …"

**1** Design a poster for a bridge competition.

**4** "You and your silly books," laughed Gaston. "I will win this contest!" Belle still thought her idea might work so she went to ask her father, the inventor.

**5**

"How about making a drawbridge?" said Belle. "You pull the ropes and the bridge goes up." "It's a splendid idea," said her father. "Let's enter the contest together!"

**6**

Belle and her father got straight to work building a miniature model bridge to show the town elders their design idea. They worked late into the night.

**2** Circle where Belle got the idea for the bridge.

a  b  c

Answer on page 69.

11

**7** Finally the day of the contest arrived! First LeFou showed his idea; a super tall bridge. "Monsieur LeFou," said a town elder, "this bridge would take me all day to climb!"

**8** Next Belle and Maurice showed their design. "This drawbridge can be opened directly from the boat." The judges studied it, but Belle still wasn't sure if they would win …

**9** Next, Gaston proposed to the town elders that they should tear down the old bridge and just let everyone swing on a rope across the river!

**3** Point to who you think should win the prize for best design.

**10** Unfortunately, Gaston didn't quite make it to the other side of the river.

**11** Finally the town elders announced their winner. "The design prize goes to ..." announced the town elder, "... Maurice and Belle!" The villagers cheered. Maurice beamed with pride. Belle felt so happy that she could use what she learned in books to help the townspeople of her village!

The End

**4** Draw a bridge across the water.

# Moonlight Memory

Belle and the Beast are dancing under the stars. Take a look at this picture for 20 seconds. Now cover it up, take the quiz and see how many you get right.

1. What colour is Belle's dress?
2. Is it sunny or is it dark?
3. Is the Beast wearing a hat?

4. How many trees did you spot?
5. Is Lumiere dancing or sleeping?

Answers on page 69.

# Brain Power

It's time for Belle's clever sudoku challenge. Can you work out which friends are missing from the grid? Write the matching numbers from the panel into the missing squares.

Each friend should only appear ONCE in each column and row!

Answer on page 69.

# Sail into ...
# Moana's World!

Even though **Moana** is warned away from the ocean, the waves call out to her. When her island is in danger, she meets a demi-god called Maui and her big ocean adventure begins.

Best friend ...
a little pig called Pua.

Loves ...
the ocean.

Secrets and dreams ...
to explore the wonders of the ocean.

Strengths ...
daring and never gives up.

The **ocean** is a **friend** of **mine**.

# Born to Voyage

Use a pencil to carefully guide Moana along the ocean path to Maui. Try to avoid touching the rocks along the way.

START

If you crash into the rocks, start again!

FINISH

# Flower Power

Te Fiti gives life to the island of Motunui. Join the dots and doodle some colourful flowers around Te Fiti.

18

# Wayfinder

Gramma Tala wants to tell Moana the secret story of her ancestors. Follow only the suns to show Moana the way to her.

START

FINISH

Answer on page 69.

# Journey to Te Fiti

The ocean is full of magic and adventure. Are you ready to play along and help the friends cross the water to reach Te Fiti?

**YOU WILL NEED:**
* 2-4 players
* a dice
* counters – you could use coins or bits of paper

**HOW TO PLAY:**
* Each player picks a friend from the **START** to guide through the ocean.
* Place your counters on the start.
* Each player takes turns to roll the dice. Move the number of spaces to match the number rolled.
* If you land on one of the **SPECIAL SPACES**, follow the instructions above.
* The first player to Te Fiti, wins!

10

11

12

9

8

13

7

14

15

5

4

16

3

17

HEIHEI

MOANA

GRAMMA TALA

START

1

2

18

PUA

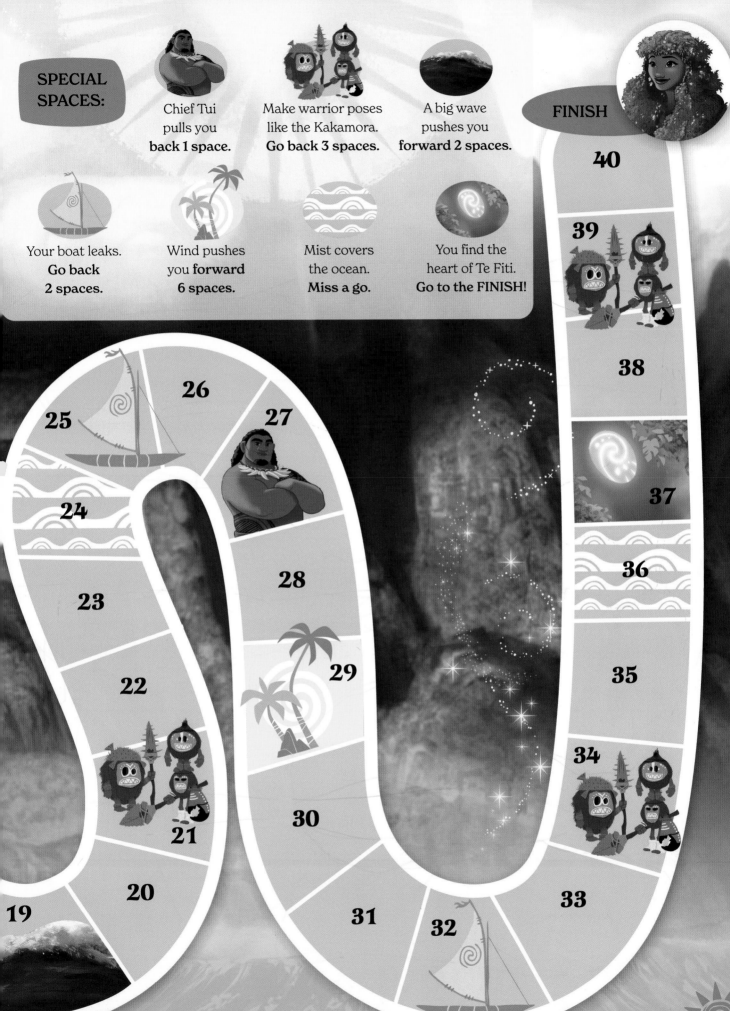

**SPECIAL SPACES:**

Chief Tui pulls you **back 1 space.**

Make warrior poses like the Kakamora. **Go back 3 spaces.**

A big wave pushes you **forward 2 spaces.**

Your boat leaks. **Go back 2 spaces.**

Wind pushes you **forward 6 spaces.**

Mist covers the ocean. **Miss a go.**

You find the heart of Te Fiti. **Go to the FINISH!**

FINISH

40
39
38
37
36
35
34
33
32
31
30
29
28
27
26
25
24
23
22
21
20
19

21

# Swing into ...
# Rapunzel's World!

After being kidnapped as a baby by Mother Gothel, **Rapunzel** is used to life locked in her tower. Until one day, when Flynn Ryder swings into her world and helps her escape. Rapunzel soon sets off on a journey to discover the secrets of her past.

## Secrets and dreams ...
to discover the mystery of the floating lights.

## Strengths ...
friendly, fun and creative.

## Best friend ...
Pascal the chameleon.

## Loves ...
painting pictures.

Make your own magic.

# Pascal in Disguise

So many Pascals! Can you spot these three Pascals hiding in the line up?

Answer on page 69.

23

# The Challenge

*When Flynn first met Rapunzel in the tower they made a deal: Flynn would take her to see the floating lanterns if she gave him back the crown he'd stolen from the castle. But now that they were out of the tower, Flynn was having second thoughts!*

**1**

Colour the floating lanterns.

**2** *"How about we have a contest?" suggested Flynn to Rapunzel. "And if I win, you give me back the crown."*

**3** *"The crown can't be part of the bet," insisted Rapunzel. Just then, Pascal's stomach growled. "Whoever loses, makes the winner a snack," suggested Rapunzel.*

**4** First, Flynn challenged Rapunzel to see who could climb a tree the fastest. "Go!" said Flynn. He quickly shot two arrows into the tree to help him climb.

**5** Flynn was sure he would win. But Rapunzel pulled herself up the tree with her hair. "What took you so long?" asked Rapunzel when Flynn reached the top.

**2**

Tick ✔ who climbed the tree fastest.

 **Flynn** ☐

 **Rapunzel** ☑

**6** But Flynn didn't think it was fair of Rapunzel to use her hair. So he wanted another contest: a race to the river! "And this time, no hair!" said Flynn.

**7** Rapunzel sped past Flynn, her hair trailing behind her. Flynn tried to speed up but he accidentally tripped over Rapunzel's hair and got completely tangled up in it.

Answer on page 69.

**8** *Rapunzel didn't realise what had happened. She kept running and sprinted to the river's edge. She had won ...*

**9** *... or so she thought. But Flynn insisted on one more contest: to get across the river! He quickly jumped in but Rapunzel couldn't swim! Luckily she got an idea when she saw Pascal hanging from a vine.*

**3** Follow the vine to help Rapunzel swing across the river.

**10** *"I don't understand," Flynn spluttered. "You got here first? And you're not even wet?" "I swung across," Rapunzel told Flynn. "You lose then because you used your hair!"*

**11** *Rapunzel showed Flynn the vine she used to swing across the river. "Fine, you win!" agreed Flynn.*

**12** "Now, you owe us a snack!" said Rapunzel. "And we're hungry, aren't we, Pascal?"

**The End**

**13** Flynn built a fire, gathered nuts and berries and cooked them up. It was delicious! "Who would have thought you might be almost as good at cooking as I am," giggled Rapunzel.

**4** Tick ✔ the biggest frying pan.

a        b        c \        d        e

Answer on page 69.

# Adventure Ready

Uh oh! The Royal Guards are looking for Flynn. Quickly guide Rapunzel through the maze to rescue her friend.

**START**

Don't bump into the guards along the way!

**FINISH**

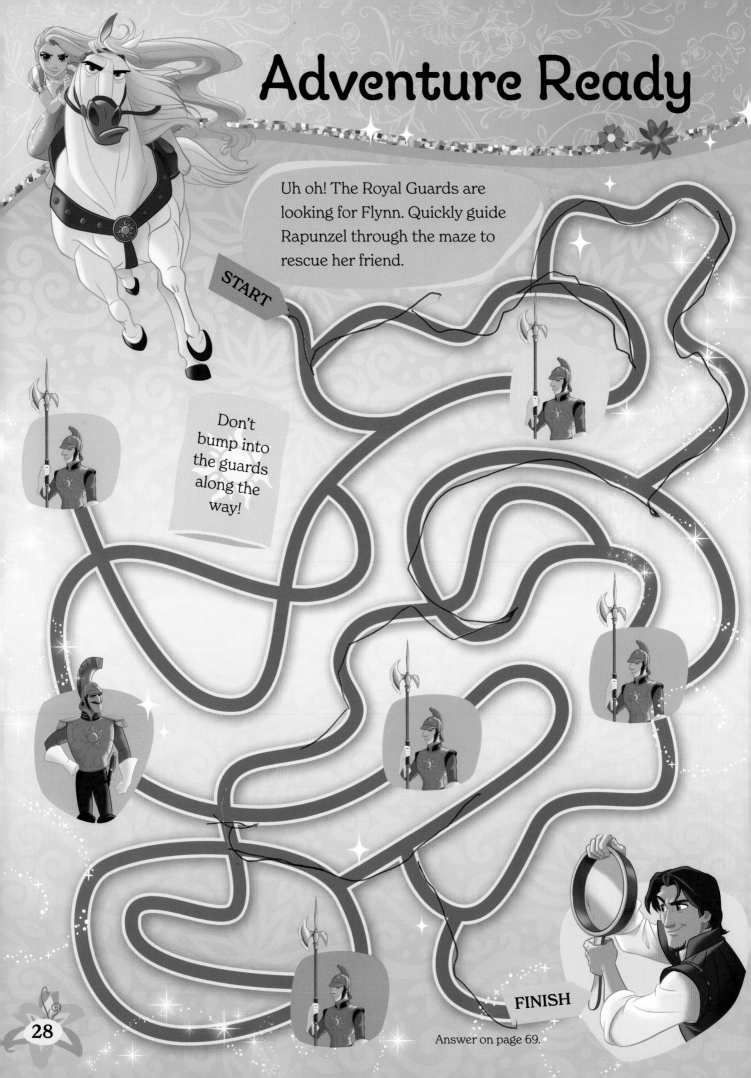

Answer on page 69.

# Dream Big

Rapunzel dreams of exploring the world. Where is your dream place to visit? Doodle it right outside Rapunzel's window.

Make your own magic!

# Fly into ...
# Jasmine's World!

Jasmine loves her father, but she feels trapped in her life. She is lonely inside the palace all day. When she meets a boy called Aladdin, she soon realises a world of magic is waiting outside the palace gates.

## Best friend ...
her pet tiger, Rajah.

## Secrets and dreams ...
to be free from the palace walls.

## Loves ...
dreaming of adventure.

## Strengths ...
curious and daring.

# Be **true** to yourself!

# Secret Shadows

Shout out **'Found you!'** each time you match a shadow.

Jasmine and her friends are playing hide-and-seek in the dark. Draw lines to match each friend to their shadow.

Answer on page 69.

# Market Mischief

Jasmine and Aladdin are looking for the magic lamp. Can you spot it?

1

These pictures look the same but there are five differences in picture 2.
Colour in a lamp each time you find a difference.

# Jasmine's Wish

Listen to this story all about Jasmine's sky-high adventure. When you see a picture, join in and say the word out loud.

 Jasmine     Abu     Aladdin     Magic Carpet     Clouds

It was morning in Agrabah and the  were dark and grey.

"Oh, I wish I could see something colourful today," sighed  .

Outside the palace,  had heard the wish. He was sure he

could find a colourful adventure for  !

Later that day,  heard a swoosh outside her window.

It was  and  on the  .

"Are you ready for a colourful adventure?" smiled  .

 ,  and  were soon all flying on the .

"It's all so wonderful!" said . But the  were

still dark and grey. Raindrops sploshed down from the sky.

,  and  giggled as they got wetter

and wetter and wetter!

"Maybe we should go home now," said . It was getting

cold. Suddenly,  jumped up and down on the .

The sun had burst through the  and a huge rainbow

filled the sky!

"My colourful wish came true!"  gasped.

 smiled. "Magic is always out there.

Sometimes it's just waiting to be found."

# Step into ...
# Cinderella's World!

When **Cinderella's** stepmother makes her work as a servant, poor Cinderella cleans and cooks all day long. Even though life is hard, Cinderella never gives up on happiness. When a Fairy Godmother appears in the night, all of Cinderella's wishes are about to come true.

Best friends ...
Jaq and Gus.

Secrets and dreams ...
to find happiness away from her home.

Loves ...
looking after her animal friends.

Strengths ...
kind and caring.

# Dreams can come true.

# Dazzling Design

Cinderella has been invited to a ball, so she needs to make a dress! Trace over the dots and add colourful patterns on her creation.

**PATTERN IDEAS**

# The Shy Princess

1 The Prince's cousin and her daughter, Princess Marie, were staying with Cinderella and the Prince. Marie was a sweet, quiet girl who was too shy to speak to Cinderella.

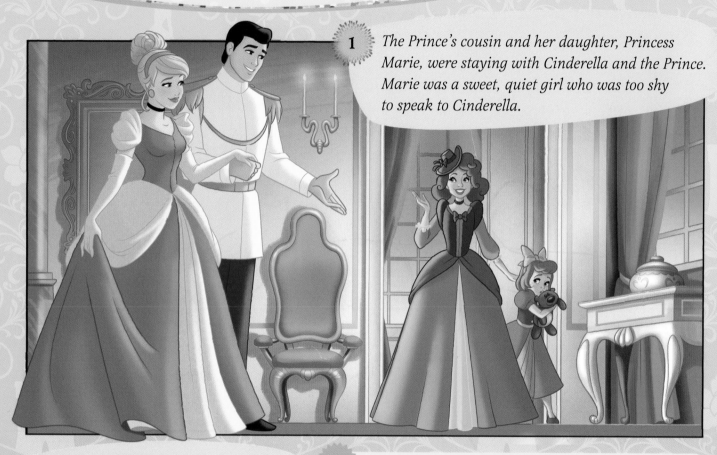

2 One day, the Prince asked Cinderella if she'd look after Marie while he and his cousin went into town. "I'm happy to help," Cinderella replied, "but she's still too shy to talk to me."

1 Spot these items in the picture above.

3 "I'm sure you'll be able to find a way to bring her out of herself," the Prince told Cinderella, fondly. Cinderella began to think of fun activities she could do with Marie.

*What would Marie like to do?*

**4** *Cinderella tried getting Marie to act out stories with her, making a treasure hunt and painting, but Marie was too shy to join in with anything.*

**5** *Gus and Jaq tried to help Cinderella by putting on an acrobatic show, but when Jaq beckoned for Marie to hold their tightrope, she shook her head.*

**2** Tick what Cinderella is painting.

 a

 b

**6** *Just then, as Jaq swung from the top of an easel, he accidentally fell and landed in a pot of paint. He wasn't hurt but was messy. "Let's get you cleaned up," said Cinderella.*

Answer on page 69.

39

**7** In the palace, Cinderella ran a bath for Jaq. As she was washing his fur, a bubble floated towards Marie. The Princess popped it and smiled shyly. This gave Cinderella an idea.

*I'm so pleased to see Marie enjoying herself.*

**8** As soon as Jaq was clean and dry, Cinderella took a bar of soap, a tray and some string into the garden. She tied the string to sticks and …

*I think Marie will like this.*

**9** … made a big bubble with soapy water. Cinderella made more bubbles and Marie began to pop them, and chase after them. Soon she was squealing with laughter. Cinderella was overjoyed to see her having so much fun.

*Thank you, Cinderella!*

**3** Circle the biggest bubble Cinderella has made.

**10** *The bubbles floated over the palace wall and a family having a picnic nearby asked if they could join in the fun. The Prince returned to see Marie happily playing with the children.*

**11** *"I knew your patience and kindness would pay off," the Prince said. Then Cinderella made the biggest bubble of the day and everybody laughed as it popped on the Prince's head!*

The End

**4** Guess who is hiding behind the bubbles.

a

b

**5** Draw another activity you think Marie would like to do.

Answer on page 69.

# Kindness Challenge

Match up the kind and helpful deeds to each princess.

**1** I can knit a scarf for you!

**2** My best friend needs a hug!

**3** Let me read you a story.

**4** I will pick strawberries for your picnic.

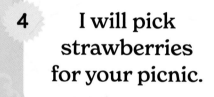

a

b

c

d

Answer on page 69.

# Kindness Quest

Now it's your turn to show the princesses all the kind things you can do too. Roll a dice and find the matching number on the wheel. Now take the quest!

Share your things.

Sing a song for your family.

Tell somebody you love them.

Paint a picture for your friends.

Help your friends.

Smile to make people happy!

1
2
3
4
5
6

# Splash into ...
# Ariel's World!

**Ariel** is warned not to go to the human world, but she just can't help herself. When she falls in love with a human prince, she is ready to risk everything for happiness – even if that means making a deal with an evil sea witch.

Best friend ...
Flounder.

Secrets and dreams ...
to live in the human world.

Strengths ...
curious and adventurous.

Loves ...
music and singing.

Find your own **voice**.

# Splash and Count

Trace over the bumpy waves and colour Ariel's tail. Now count her underwater friends! Point to your answer in the number line.

Can you draw 5 more splashy sea creatures?

0 1 2 3 4 5 6 7 8 9 10

Answer on page 69.

# Treasure Trail

Ariel and Flounder have found an old treasure map. Guide them through the maze to a secret treasure chest.

START

FINISH

Answer on page 69.

# Splashy Sequences

It is always busy under the sea. Study the patterns below and draw in the missing picture in each row.

**1**

**2**

**3**

Answer on page 69.

47

# Ariel as Queen

**1** Spot the odd one out.

a   b   c

**1** One day, Ariel was so busy exploring a shipwreck that she missed dinner. Her father, King Triton, led a search party to find her.

**2** Ariel had been distracted by a pretty brooch which glowed with magic.

*You've missed dinner!*

**3** King Triton was angry that Ariel had broken the rule to always be on time for dinner.

**Rules are …**

**Rules are …**

**4** "What a fussy rule," Ariel insisted, "I'd never make silly rules if I was in charge!" Then both Ariel and King Triton spoke at the same time and the brooch glowed brightly.

**5** The magical brooch made Ariel and the King swap places! Now Ariel was the Queen of Atlantica and Triton was just a handsome young prince.

**6** When Ariel returned to the palace it was as if she had always been queen! Young Prince Triton was left to explore the sea.

**7** Without the King's rules in place, everything seemed to go wrong. Chariots went the wrong way and crashed into each other.

**8** People argued with one another, music played too loudly, and no one listened to anyone else.

**8** Ariel was relieved when teatime came and she didn't have to make any more rules for the day. But Triton was nowhere to be found.

**9** Ariel led a search party to find the missing young prince who was really her father.

*Where is he?*

*The shipwreck - of course!*

**10** They found Triton in the old shipwreck where he was sorting through treasures.

**11** "Being the ruler isn't as easy as I expected," Ariel admitted.

**12** "Your rules aren't so fussy after all," Ariel said, hugging her father. As they hugged, magic filled the air once more.

**13** A moment later, they were back to their old selves and the brooch had disappeared. "I make my rules because I care so much about you," King Triton said.

*I love you.*

**14** "I know," Ariel told him, "and I wouldn't have it any other way."

*I love you, too!*

The End

**2** Count the colourful fish.

[ ] fish

Answer on page 69.

# Jump into ...
# Mulan's World!

When **Mulan** disguises herself as a man to take her father's place in the war, she is more than ready to battle for her family. Luckily, Mulan soon finds even the Imperial Army are no match for her cunning warrior skills!

## Best friend ...
Mushu.

## Secrets and dreams ...
to bring happiness to her family.

## Strengths ...
brave warrior skills.

## Loves ...
to fight for what she believes in.

Be **True** to your **heart!**

# Warrior Workout

Mulan is practising her warrior moves. Draw lines to match her fierce poses into pairs.

1

2

3

4

5

Now pick a move
and try it yourself.
Practice makes perfect!

6

7

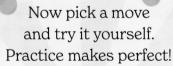

8

Answer on page 69.

# Princess Power

Grab your crayons and give this picture some princess power!

Be your own hero!

# The Race Home

Mulan is racing home to see her family. Tick the boxes when you spot the close-ups in the big picture.

**1**

**2**

**3**

**4**

**5**

Answer on page 69.

# Skip into ...
# Aurora's World!

After an evil curse is cast on **Aurora** as a baby, she is sent to live with three fairies in the forest. Aurora is happy for a time until she learns of her curse and her peaceful life is about to change forever.

**Best friends ...**
all the creatures in the forest!

**Secrets and dreams ...**
to find true love and happiness.

**Loves ...**
singing to her animal friends.

**Strengths ...**
kind and gentle.

## Always be kind.

# Animal Friends

All of the forest animals love playing with Aurora. Now you can play along too. Take this fun quiz all about lots of creatures she knows.

**1** Point to the animal that can **fly**.

a  b  c

**2** Point to the **BIGGEST** creature.

a  b

c

**3** Point to the **smallest** friend.

a

b

c

Answer on page 69.

57

# Wonderful World

Up in the clouds, the good fairies have cast a spell. Words all about Aurora have appeared in the sky.

Trace over the words with a pencil to bring them to life.

Which of these words best describes you?

kind

happy

caring

brave

# Forest Fun

Aurora is teaching the animals to swirl and twirl!
Use your happiest colours to fill the picture with fun.

# Leap into ...
# Tiana's World!

**Tiana** loves to cook and has big dreams to share her food with the world! She works hard and has no time for anything else. Everything changes when she turns into a frog and learns that maybe work isn't the only thing in life after all.

### Best friend ...
Lottie La Bouff.

### Secrets and dreams ...
to buy her own restaurant.

### Loves ...
cooking, singing and music.

### Strengths ...
works hard and doesn't give up.

# Light the way to your dreams!

# Go Green

There are lots of green and magical things in Tiana's world. Can you spot and circle all the green pictures below?

1

2

3

4

5

6

7

8

9

10

Answer on page 69.

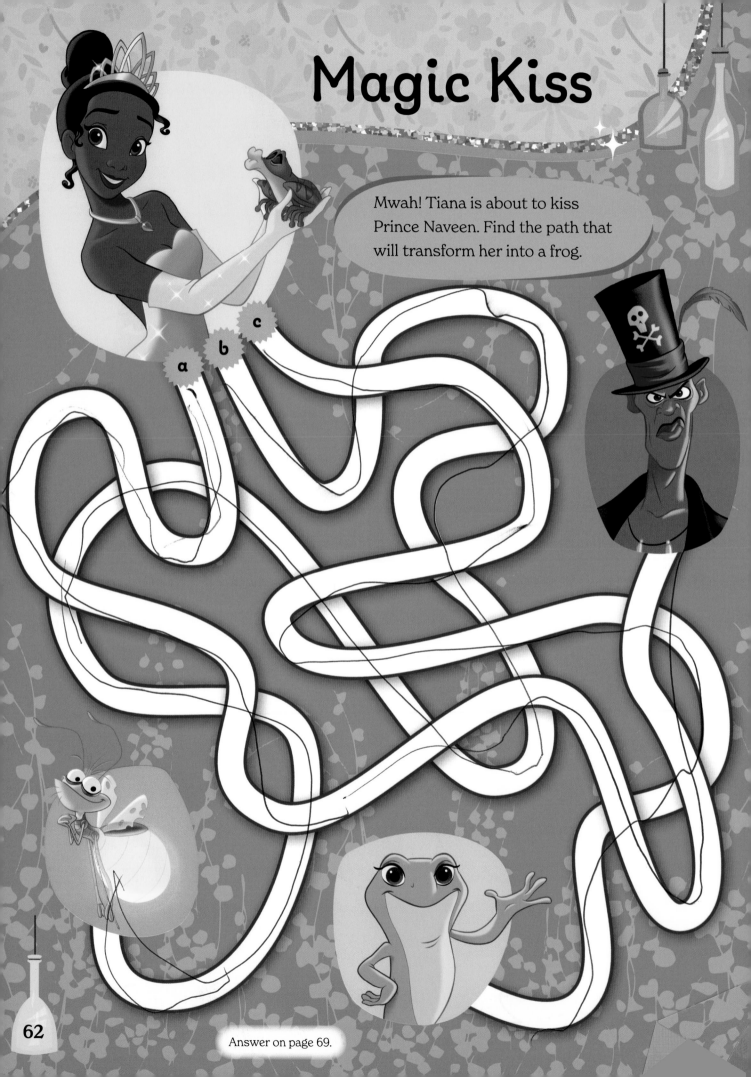

# Magic Kiss

Mwah! Tiana is about to kiss Prince Naveen. Find the path that will transform her into a frog.

# Tick, Tock, Go!

Every day is a busy day for Tiana. Follow her from morning to night and draw in the clock hands as you go.

**Good morning!**
It's time for work.

8 o'clock

**Lunch!**
Tiana picks yummy food to eat.

1 o'clock

**Play!**
Tiana takes a break to play tennis.

3 o'clock

**Night-time!**
Tiana swirls and twirls until the stars shine.

9 o'clock

# Which Princess Are You?

Play along and take the quiz to find out which princess you are most like.

**1** My favourite thing to do is:

**a** Go for a swim    **b** Read a book    **c** Paint a picture    **d** Bake something

**2** I'd like to live:

**a** by the sea

**b** in a small town

**c** in a tower

**d** in a big city

**3** My favourite colour is:

**a** blue    **b** yellow

**c** purple    **d** green

64

**4** My favourite animal friend is:

 a     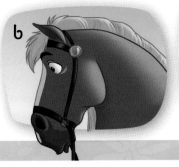 b      c      d

**5** The best word to describe you is:

a adventurous     b clever     c fun     d determined

## Mostly **a**s:
### You are Ariel
You are a singing star, full of fun and adventure. When you're not discovering new things, you love to play and dance with your friends and family.

## Mostly **b**s:
### You are Belle
You love reading books all about the world and are always bursting with new ideas. When your family needs help with anything, you are the one to call!

## Mostly **c**s:
### You are Rapunzel
You are never far from your paints and your amazing art covers your walls. Fun and active, you can often be found climbing trees and swinging around!

## Mostly **d**s:
### You are Tiana
No challenge is too big for you. You work, work, work to get what you want. When you do find time to relax, you love to bake treats for your friends.

# Magical Seasons

**Snow, sun, flowers and fun ...**
Each season is full of adventure. Trace over the words under each picture to spell out the seasons.

Spring

Summer

Autumn

Winter

# Change
## your
# World!

© Disney

**Be Yourself!**

# Answers

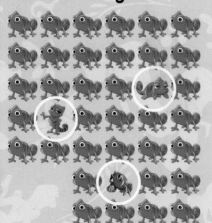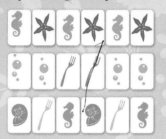